OCTOBRIANA
NEO—PULP

By David Eveleigh

Copyright 2021 David Eveleigh

While some controversy exists surrounding Octobriana's original authorship, all those credited with creating her have openly expressed that she is a public domain character. Anyone may use her, for any purpose.

"The Claw" is the creation of Jack Cole for Lev Gleason Publications and is also public domain.

In keeping with the tradition and spirit of these fine characters, the author wishes to let it be known that all the new characters created for this book are also free for anyone to use. If you wish to create your own sequel, go right ahead.

Dedicated to independent creators everywhere, regardless of their political stripes.

Nobody knows for sure. Some say that she was an Amazon warrior from an advanced ancient civilization and that she was made immortal by an experimental radiation treatment. Others claim that she is the spirit of the October Revolution, whose values were betrayed by the Soviet government, and that she has simply always existed. Whatever the case, she captains the Wonder Machine, travelling back and forth through time and space, fighting against tyranny wherever she finds it. These are her adventures...

With a medical mask covering the lower half of her face, the tall blond woman stalked through the nearly abandoned shopping mall. In her many centuries of life, she had never faced an enemy she could not defeat. Until now. The virus had decimated global economies. Capitalist or socialist, the disease took no sides.

Western songs with lyrics that reminded her of the glorious revolution filled the air. There were a lot of songs like that lately. Movies too. And...

Books?

Her eyes fell on the front window of Tchort's Book Shop. There, she saw her face reflected on the cover of a strange novel.

Octobriana: Neo-Pulp.

She cocked her head to one side.

That's me, she thought. Indeed, there was no denying it. From the iconic red star on her forehead to the black snake wrapped around her left wrist, it was her. It had to be her.

Octobriana washed her hands and entered the store. She was greeted cordially by a tall, thin man with slicked-back silver hair. He could have been mistaken for an undertaker were it not for the Mickey Mouse mask that he wore to protect himself from the plague.

"Ah, hello," he said, "is there anything I can help you with?"

"That book," Octobriana said, pointing.

The Mickey Mouse man picked up the book in question and admired the cover.

"Oh yes, the 'Spirit of the October Revolution'. They don't make superheroes like her anymore."

The real Octobriana didn't notice the compliment. She was too hypnotized by her own likeness, reproduced for mass consumption, to pay attention.

"Do you not find it strange that such a symbol of communist ideals should be adopted for consumerism?" She asked.

"All existence is consumerist," he said, "if we cease to consume, we cease to exist. The kind of freedom she fought for originally doesn't exist and never will."

"Only someone who has never had to fight for their freedom would think that way."

"Here, take a look inside and tell me I'm wrong."

He handed her the book. Octobriana began flipping through the pages when a strange sensation overcame her. When a person reads a book, it is common for them to visualize what is being described. But her visualizations were becoming flesh. The descriptions materialized before her. When she realized what was happening, it was too late. She screamed as she disappeared from the real world and entered the world of the printed page.

The Mickey Mouse man watched her vanish, then picked up the book and put it back in the window.

"At last, Octobriana, I'm finally rid of you."

I

Ukraine, 1959...

The metal cylinder containing Comrade Stalin's brain glistened as the car passed a dim, yellow street lamp. General Malik repressed a shudder and glanced at the container. He had endured many horrors in the name of the Soviet Union, nothing compared to this... this... *thing.*

"Is something wrong, Comrade?" The brain said through an electronic voice box. Malik always thought that it sounded dry and static, as if it could be anybody's mind contained within. The driver stopped at a red light, prolonging the ride.

"Nothing at all," he replied, "just the cold."

"Ah yes," the brain said, "the cold. I have forgotten what it feels like."

"Don't you feel anything, Comrade?"

"Not a thing."

Silence descended on the car. The light ahead turned green and the journey resumed. Before long, they were parked in front of the October Palace. The building had been damaged severely during the war and restorations were still underway. However, there was a secret chamber below the wreckage. One that the current leaders knew nothing about.

General Malik, ever loyal, picked up the cylinder and carried it into the ruin. Downwards they went. Sweat formed on the general's hands. He hoped that this *thing* would approve of what he had to show it.

Doctor Dimension, wearing her red and blue D-Goggles which let her see through time and space, greeted them as they entered the secret chamber. She grinned, obviously very pleased with herself. Malik did not share her optimism.

"Gentlemen," she said in English, "welcome. Tell me, what has been the number one obstacle we've faced in restoring Comrade Stalin to power?"

"Octobriana," the electronic voice hissed.

"Not anymore," the doctor replied. She gestured to a red curtain at the far end of the chamber.

"Thanks to a single drop of blood obtained during your last battle with her, I have created the ultimate weapon."

Doctor Dimension walked over to the curtain and drew it aside. What stood behind it shocked Malik to his core.

It was Octobriana.

Only she was changed. Her hair had turned black, a white snake was wrapped around her right wrist and the red star on her forehead was gone. In its place were a hammer and a sickle. The sign of the CCCP.

"Comrades," the doctor said, "allow me to

introduce Antiana. With my goggles, I can track Octobriana. With Antiana's strength and skill, we can crush her once and for all!"

Antiana stepped forward.

"For Comrade Stalin and the communist state, I will kill the spirit of revolution by any means necessary."

II

From inside the gulag, everything looked bleak. The barracks were like tombs. Even the snow somehow seemed grey. Any semblance of freedom lay beyond the barbed wire barrier. And even if someone could get past it, where would they go?

Alexei's emaciated frame tumbled to the ground as the butt of the guard's gun hit him in the back of the head. He heard the rifle click and expected the end. What he didn't expect was a total solar eclipse.

Both Alexei and the guard looked up to see a strange spherical object blocking out the sun. It was black all over, save for a large red star emblazoned on the front.

"The Wonder Machine!" The guard stammered, "Octobriana is here!"

Indeed she was! Before Alexei could even process the guard's words, the latter was lying in a pool of blood next to him. A woman's silhouette approached. She knelt and offered her hand, which Alexei accepted. He had not seen a woman in years, let alone one as radiant as the Slavic Superwoman.

Other guards rushed her, but were cut down by machine gun fire from the Wonder Machine. The Russian she-devil drew her Smith & Wesson revolver and picked off her remaining opponents. Just as she drew a breath of relief, the ground began to rumble.

"Oh no," Alexei said, "they've started the

Under Machine."

"The Under Machine?" Octobriana queried.

"It's what they've had us building here," Alexei replied, "some general's orders."

He did not have a chance to explain further.

It started as just a tiny pyramid peeking out from beneath the snow. But that was only the tip. The earth shook so violently that both Alexei and his rescuer lost their footing. They could only watch as an immense, trapezoidal drill burst from beneath the surface. Octobriana's eyes widened at the sight. A doorway opened in the side and a small battalion of soldiers emerged from the towering structure, led by a woman who could have been Octobriana's sister.

Except for the mark on her forehead.

Antiana grinned. Her soldiers aimed their rifles at the hapless duo and...

Bang!

Antiana had forgotten about the Wonder Machine. Its guns blazed, cutting down half her army in mere seconds. Octobriana took advantage of her clone's momentary confusion and pounced on her with the fury of a tigress. The soldiers fled for cover and tried firing back helplessly at their hovering attacker. And poor Alexei? Well, he could only watch.

Watch as the Russian she-devil tangled with her opponent.

Watch as Antiana wrapped her arm around Octobriana's throat.

Watch as his savior's neck began to crack.

Alexei had to do something. He grabbed the

dead guard's rifle and...

Blam!

Antiana's head exploded. Her would-be victim took deep breaths as she found her footing again. Within seconds, the Russian she-devil was ready to fight again.

But it turned out that no further fighting was necessary that day. Under the onslaught of the Wonder Machine, the rest of the soldiers either retreated or surrendered to their new mistress.

Octobriana smiled and pointed towards the black sphere in the sky.

"Do you know who pilots that?" She asked rhetorically, "indigenous people from all over the world who elected to join me in my fight against tyranny. That's why we're going to win this revolution."

She regarded her clone's corpse for a second.

"She only had the state on her side."

The mystery woman known only as Octobriana put a hand on Alexei's shoulder and looked him happily in the eyes.

"I have the people on mine."

I

Eastern Europe, sometime in the Dark Ages...

The sun rose over Princess Mia's Disneyland kingdom for the last time. Of course, when she woke that morning, she didn't know that it would be the last time. No, she expected that her reign over this land would last forever. It was a beautiful morning too. She gazed out her bedroom window and admired the view. Her rule extended well into the horizon, where the sun touched the mountains.

In the streets below, the little people were just starting to stir. Workers, housewives, children, all rose to greet the new day.

There was a knock at the princess's door. Curious, who could want her at this hour?

"Who is it?" She asked.

"Your highness," said a familiar voice.

"Come in, Sister."

The door opened and in stepped a young nun. Sister Salvation.

"We found a witch in the city," the nun said, "she says that she represents the Knights Templar."

"That's impossible," Mia said, "the Templars are extinct."

"I know," Sister Salvation replied, "I was there the day that they were burned. I saw their idols of Baphomet and heard them pray to the Great Old Ones. But this witch, she insists that she is here on their behalf."

Mia's eyebrow raised.

"Where is she?"

"In the dungeon," the nun said, "awaiting her trial."

"Take me to her."

II

Octobriana had to confess that there was a lapse in her memory. She didn't remember travelling back to the Dark Ages. Had the Wonder Machine brought her here? The last thing she could remember was...

"At last, Octobriana, I'm finally rid of you."

Why did that sound familiar?

The mission! Of course she could remember her mission here. Princess Mia was renowned throughout history. But there was a cost to her lavish lifestyle. Wealth only exists in finite amounts, after all. While she sang her life away behind the palace gates, the working people of her kingdom starved.

Octobriana struggled with her bonds, but it was no use. She was strapped quite securely to the rack.

The door to the torture chamber opened and in stepped two young women. She recognized the nun from earlier, but the other was unfamiliar. However, judging by how expensive her clothes looked, the Soviet Wonder Woman was willing to bet that this was Princess Mia herself.

"Who are you?" The princess asked. Sister Salvation cranked the rack a notch and Octobriana's bonds tightened. She resisted the pain, but spoke anyway. She had a message to deliver.

"I am the spirit of revolution. Just as the Knights Templar burned, so too shall I see you burn."

"But we have done nothing," Sister Salvation said, "this kingdom is the happiest place on earth."

"Tell that to all the other witches you've tortured. No, the people are only happy because they are afraid to be anything else."

Mia turned her back to Octobriana.

"In an hour," the princess said, "you will stand trial for witchcraft and heresy. May God have mercy on your soul."

"I don't need his mercy."

III

There were once many methods of determining whether someone was a witch. One of the most popular was to bind the hands and feet of the accused and throw them into a large body of water. If they drowned, they were deemed innocent and given a proper Christian burial. But if they survived, it was believed that it could only be because the Devil had rescued them. Thus, they would be promptly burned at the stake.

Sister Salvation stood behind the Red Templar as they both stood on the edge of a cliff facing the ocean. This mystery woman with a star on her forehead showed no emotion as her hands and feet were bound by the palace guards.

"This is your last chance," the nun said, "if you confess your sins now, you may be granted salvation in the afterlife."

"I don't need salvation," the Red Templar replied, "I shall not repent."

"As you please."

As soon as the she-devil was properly bound, Sister Salvation pushed her and watched her plummet.

Splash!

The Red Templar disappeared beneath the waves. At first, the nun wondered if she had been wrong. Perhaps the Devil would not rescue this mystery woman.

However, her initial suspicions proved to have been well founded.

The sinister sister watched as the ocean

opened up and a massive black sphere emerged from the depths. It bore the same sigil as the Red Templar.

The five-pointed star.

The mark of the beast.

The devil woman rode the sphere as it ascended into the heavens, as if to challenge the supremacy of God, wielding weapons that the nun had never even imagined before. Looking at her, Sister Salvation couldn't help but wonder...

Was this the entity that the Knights Templar had called Baphomet?

IV

The Russian she-devil rode the Wonder Machine up to Princess Mia's palace. She had another message to deliver. Not to the princess this time, but to the people. As she spoke, the Wonder Machine amplified her voice so that it could be heard far and wide.

"To the workers of the so-called 'happiest place on earth'. All is not right in your magic kingdom. While you scrape for food, the princess lives a life of luxury. While you starve, she persecutes you with endless witch hunts. You don't need to pretend to be happy. Why be happy when there is something deeply wrong? You stand at a crossroads in history. You can either side with your fairytale princess and share her fate or you can turn your back on her and seek your own fortune. The decision is yours. Octobriana has spoken."

She watched from above as the little people discussed among themselves. The decision seemed unanimous. Even the guards threw down their weapons and joined the mass exodus from Disneyland. Octobriana smiled. The people had won again.

Well, not yet.

The Russian she-devil looked up to Princess Mia's bedroom window. There, Sister Salvation glared at her angrily. The nasty nun leapt onto the Wonder Machine with a sword in her hands.

"You shall not triumph, Baphomet," she said, "I have God on my side."

"God is not here," Octobriana replied, "there

is only me."

The Red Templar aimed her Smith & Wesson and fired.

Blam!

Blam!

Blam!

With expert swordsmanship, Sister Salvation deflected the bullets. Octobriana raised an eyebrow, holstered her gun and drew her dagger.

This should prove interesting.

The nasty nun lunged at the Russian she-devil and...

Slash!

Her blade narrowly missed Octobriana's head. The spirit of revolution swiped with her dagger and...

Clink!

The two blades met and locked together. Sister Salvation pushed against her opponent and Octobriana pushed back. Little by little, the sword inched towards the Russian she-devil's throat.

Wham!

Octobriana kicked her enemy in the stomach. Sister Salvation lost her footing and slid down the side of the Wonder Machine. She tried to get a grip, but the surface was too smooth. The nasty nun screamed all the way down until...

Thud!

"Tell me, Sister," Octobriana said, "where will you be spending eternity?"

She studied the castle and saw Princess Mia peering out from the bedroom window. The time had come.

The Wonder Machine powered up its atomic heat ray and...

Zap!

The once beautiful palace was reduced to ashes.

I

USSR, 1990...

The Siberian Tundra is a notoriously cold place. General Malik noted that, even through his gloves, the chill from the metal cylinder in his hands made his fingers numb. He and the brain contained within that cylinder oversaw the work detail, who broke their backs digging through the snow and ice.

"My patience with this project is wearing thin," said an electronic voice which emanated from the cylinder, "are you sure we're digging in the right spot?"

"Absolutely," Malik replied, "Doctor Dimension's D-Goggles detected our prize in this location. According to her, we should be right on top of..."

One of the men cried out.

"What is it?" The electronic voice demanded.

"They've found something."

The general carried the metal cylinder down into the work area. The men were thin and ready to collapse, but he paid no heed. He was too hypnotized by what they had found.

Visible beneath the ice was a bony, green hand, large enough to crush a tank in its cruel grip. Malik smiled at the sight.

Release me, said a voice inside his head. He turned and faced the workers.

"None of you are to sleep until this is free from the ice," he said, "is that clear?"

"Please," one of the men said, "we haven't eaten or rested in days..."

"And would you like to explain to Comrade Stalin here why you should be allowed to stop now that victory is so near?"

The worker turned his eyes downwards.

"What is that thing?" He asked, "the Devil?"

"No," the electronic voice answered, "the Claw."

II

Yes, the Claw! That strange invader from the planet Zylmarx was ready to rear his hideous head once again. Although trapped beneath the Siberian ice, he sent telepathic signals throughout the globe telling his loyal, goblin-like clawites to prepare for his return. On the Pacific island of Ricca, they celebrated with human sacrifices to their God of Hate.

For wherever there is hate, the Claw lives!

All his old enemies were dust now. The world was finally safe for dictators.

Word began to spread across the globe. From Tibet to the Koreas, a shudder of fear quaked through Asia like a tremor. For no people knew of the Claw's cruelty more than those who had borne it.

But in the mind of General Malik, the Claw was not cruel at all. He thought back to his youth in the monster's employ; the magnificent dreams, each one sweeter than the last, which the beast from Zylmarx had given him through telepathy. How he'd grown addicted to those dreams. How he longed to experience them once again.

The full moon rose over Siberia and a trio of sinister figures watched the excavation. The bony, green hand was now fully unearthed and, as the light stretched over it, it began to move.

"What's happening?" Doctor Dimension asked as the ground rumbled.

"Armageddon!" Answered Malik. The Earth shook and the ice cracked. A gigantic figure in green emerged from underneath and stretched itself upwards to challenge heaven. It looked down on General Malik, Doctor Dimension and Stalin's brain with a hideous face like a shriveled, hairless cat.

"I live again!" Bellowed the Claw, "you three shall be rewarded. But I must ask,... why? Why did you release me from the ice?"

"I propose a bargain," said Stalin's brain, "Comrade Claw, if you will bring Moscow to its knees for me, I will ensure that Mother Russia provides you with all the slaves you will ever need."

The Claw stroked his chin.

"Your offer pleases me," he said, "it is agreed then. Before the sun sets tomorrow, Moscow will be yours!"

III

It had been such a peaceful evening in Moscow. The sun had set and the full moon was just beginning to cast its glow. In the Kremlin, the supreme leader was lying in bed next to his wife. A well-read copy of *Kapital* rested in his hands and his eyes scanned the pages hungrily.

"Do you hear that sound?" His wife asked. The leader listened. Indeed, there was a soft, whisper of a voice talking to him.

"I hear, master," he said, "and I obey!"

The next morning, he surprised everyone by calling a press conference. Every member of the media waited with bated breath as he took the podium.

"My friends," the supreme leader said, "as of this moment, I relinquish my command and hereby name the Claw as my successor."

IV

Malik's back ached as he dug through the ice. He wasn't a general anymore, just a lowly soldier again. Less than a soldier, really. Comrade Stalin felt that the Claw had betrayed them. He would feel that way, even though the God of Hate had decided to let him live as an advisor. Malik and Doctor Dimension, meanwhile, had been put to work with the rest of the populace, unearthing the Zylmarx invasion fleet, which was still frozen beneath the Siberian snow. It was hard work, but it was worth it to have the dreams again. Every day, he grew thinner and paler. But every night, the dreams became more fantastic and wonderful. For them, the pain in his back and the emptiness in his belly could be tolerated.

Malik had to admit it, he was not a young man anymore. He doubted that he would survive this ordeal.

He prayed to the God of Hate that he would at least die in his sleep, amongst those sweet, sweet dreams.

V

But don't worry, oh ever patient reader, we have not forgotten about Octobriana. This is her book after all.

The Russian she-devil had just finished thwarting the Draculoids' invasion of Pluto and was heading back to Earth for some rest and relaxation (and maybe a Coke). She was still disturbed by the gap in her memory. It was starting to clear though. She could remember an old man and something about a book shop. But who was he? That question would have to wait. Because as soon as the Wonder Machine entered Earth's atmosphere, its sensors picked up strange readings from below.

"Octobriana," one of the crew said, "there is something wrong down there. It,... it can't be! The Claw has returned!"

A chill went up the Soviet Wonder Woman's spine. The Claw!? It was impossible! She had sealed him and his invasion fleet beneath the Siberian ice. But, like a bad penny, he just kept coming back.

"Where is he?" She asked. The crewman's face went pale when he saw what the sensors had to say.

"According to our scans, the Kremlin. And according to all media broadcasts, he has successfully conquered the USSR."

"And it's only a matter of time before he launches an assault on the rest of the world," Octobriana said, "set a course for the Kremlin. It's time we buried him once and for all."

VI

The Claw had always coveted Earth. His own planet was notably quite poor. But Earth was wealthy beyond belief. Soon that wealth would belong to Zylmarx. But he had to work fast. After all, his demonic powers were linked to the phases of the moon. The light of the full moon had resurrected him, but a moonless night was coming soon, which would temporarily rob him of his otherworldly abilities. That's why he needed his fleet. If the earthmen learned of his weakness, they would surely overthrow him.

The God of Hate leaned back in his fiery throne. On a footstool next to him was the metal cylinder which contained Stalin's brain. He could sense the former dictator's frustration telepathically and that torment amused him to no end. But, like all good things, the Claw's amusement wasn't meant to last.

There was a disturbance in his nation. He could sense it. Something had come from out of the sky.

"Octobriana!" He said. His amusement from a moment before turned into fear and then into rage. So, the Soviet Wonder Woman had come to challenge him again. This time, he would be the one to bury her and her descendants would be raised under the banner of the Claw.

The God of Hate sent out a psychic signal, mobilizing the entire army and air force. They had one order: *Shoot down the Wonder Machine!*

Brainwashed soldiers marched by the

thousands through the streets of Moscow, while tanks and planes converged to meet Octobriana head on. However, no matter how much firepower they launched in its direction, they simply could not penetrate the Wonder Machine's force field.

As the Claw paced angrily about his throne room, Stalin's brain remained calm and collected.

"Why don't you use nuclear weapons against her?" The electronic voice asked. The Claw stopped pacing and turned angrily to the metal cylinder.

"And destroy the country which I fought so hard to conquer?" He said, "never! Bah! It seems I shall have to deal with Octobriana myself!"

VII

Inside the Wonder Machine, the crew was scrambling to keep the ship afloat. You couldn't tell from the outside, but the constant barrage on the force field was draining their energy supply. In a little while, the Wonder Machine would be too weak to maintain the shields, then everybody aboard would be in danger.

Octobriana remained stern throughout the assault. The Slavic Superwoman waited ever so patiently.

"Shouldn't we fire back?" Said one of the crew.

"No," Octobriana replied, "they should stop soon."

Sure enough, all the shooting ended abruptly.

"See?" She said, "Comrade Claw was never the patient type. Now, if I'm right, he should be coming to greet us himself."

Within seconds, the ship's sensors detected a gigantic figure approaching from the Kremlin.

"It's him," the Russian she-devil said. She closed her eyes and, knowing he could read her mind, thought out a message for the God of Hate.

I know you can hear this, she thought, *if we fight here and now, it will only cause more death and destruction. So, I'm giving you this one chance; leave this beautiful country and its people alone. Otherwise, I will kill you.*

The Claw laughed so loud that she could hear it from inside the Wonder Machine.

"Do your worst," he bellowed, "I've died a

thousand times before, but I always come back. Nothing can kill the Claw!"

Scrape!

He raked his talons against the side of the Wonder Machine. The ship shook and its lights flickered.

Scrape!

Scrape!

"Back up," Octobriana ordered her crew, "get us out of his reach."

The Wonder Machine rose high into the air, far away from the Claw's grasp.

"Now," she said, "charge the atomic heat ray and fire the machine guns."

Rattattattattat!

All guns roared to life, spitting death at their target. However, the bullets only seemed to make the God of Hate angrier.

"The machine guns have no effect," said one of the crew.

"Is the heat ray charged?" Octobriana asked. The crewman nodded. The Russian she-devil smiled.

"Give him hell!"

Zap!

The atomic heat ray hit the Claw directly in the chest. It pushed him backwards into a nearby skyscraper, which collapsed on top of him with a thunderous...

Crash!

"Did that do it?" Asked one of the crew, "is he dead?"

There was a moment of stillness as the smoke

cleared. There didn't seem to be any trace of the God of Hate. But the moment was disturbed by a signal on the control panel.

"There's a message," Octobriana said, "punch it through."

On the viewing screen in front of her, Octobriana saw the metal cylinder which contained Stalin's brain.

"Congratulations," it said in a flat, electronic voice, "you've done what Daredevil and the Ghost couldn't do. You've successfully destroyed the Claw! As a reward for your efforts, I'm sending a surprise your way, courtesy of Polaris."

The screen went blank.

"Octobriana," one of the crew said, "our sensors tell us that a nuclear missile has just been launched and is heading in our direction."

The Slavic Superwoman swore.

"How much power do we have left for the force field?" She asked.

"Not much."

"It'll have to do. Take us to that missile."

"But,..."

"Now!"

The crew leapt into action and, in the blink of an eye, the Wonder Machine was on its way. Travelling at supersonic speed, it reached the errant nuclear device in no time.

"Okay," Octobriana said, "project the force field around the missile."

The crew obeyed and, within seconds, the bomb was caught inside a bubble of energy.

"It's getting ready to detonate," one of the

crew said.

"Redirect its course," Octobriana said, "send it straight up."

The rocket turned upward in midair as the seconds counted down.

"Now," the Russian she-devil said, "drop the shield."

The force field vanished and the missile shot up into space where...

Kaboom!

It exploded harmlessly amongst the stars.

VIII

Malik was happy to be a general again. He was even happier that the Claw's body had not been found. The rubble had been cleared and, yet, it simply had not been there. Some claimed that the heat ray must have vaporized it, but Malik knew the truth. The God of Hate was still alive. He'd return someday when the world least expected it. How did Malik know? Whenever he fell asleep, he still had those wonderful dreams.

All he had to do was wait.

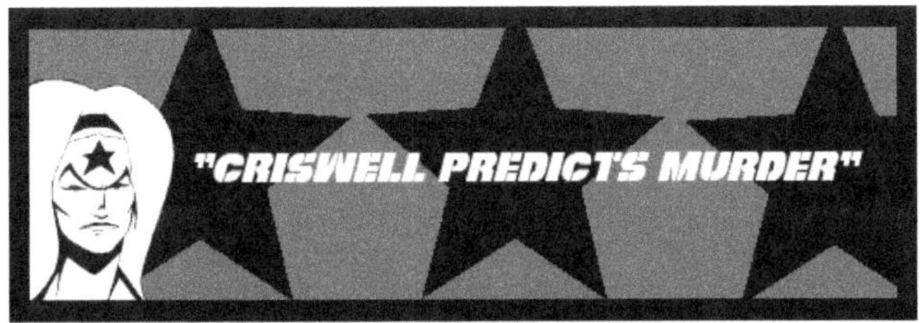

I

Somewhere in the mists of time and space...
It must be great to get paid to be wrong all the time.

That's what Achak thought about the media.

Working in the lower decks of the Wonder Machine, it was his job to monitor broadcasts from across time and space. If anything seemed strange or, at least, strange by the media's standards, he would report it to Octobriana, who would investigate it. His job wasn't bad. In fact, the Soviet Wonder Woman was the ideal boss. You didn't work for her, you worked *with* her. She was no stranger to the lower decks either. Often, he would see her walking amongst the crew, always with an approving nod or smile. And not just to Achak. Everyone on board was equally important in her eyes.

He leaned back in his chair as the intro to his favorite program began.

Criswell Predicts was an American television series from 1953, starring Jeron Criswell King, aka The Amazing Criswell. With a face that was made in America, the renowned psychic took center stage as the camera focused on him. He began to rattle off a series of prophecies that he claimed would befall the human race in the twentieth century.

"I predict that a ray from outer space will turn all the world's metal into rubber!" He said. Achak smiled. Surely nobody actually believed this guy. Still, there was something off about Criswell tonight. Something that the lowly operator of the Wonder Machine couldn't put his finger on.

"I predict," the psychic said, "that on August twenty-fifth, 1967, George Lincoln Rockwell will be assassinated. You may have heard of the assassin. Her name is Octobriana!"

Achak raised an eyebrow. Now that was strange by the media's standards.

II

For those of you who don't know, George Lincoln Rockwell was the founder of the American Nazi Party. In fact, if the rise of Neo-Nazism can be attributed to anybody after World War II, he would bear sole credit. And on August 25th, 1967, he waited nervously inside his Hatenanny bus out in the middle of nowhere. His loyal stormtroopers stood guard outside and he had a few surprises of his own for any would-be assassins. But none of that prevented his hand from shaking as he poured himself a drink. Just one small drink to steady his nerves.

Then came the sound...

Crack!

There was no mistaking it. That was a gunshot.

Rockwell picked up his walkie-talkie and barked into it.

"What's going on out there?" He demanded.

"We've spotted someone," a nervous voice replied, "it looks like a woman."

That must be Octobriana, Rockwell thought.

"She ducked into the woods," the voice continued, "shall we go after her."

"No," the American Fuhrer said, "unleash Supremasaurus."

"Are you sure? We haven't fully trained him yet."

"Just do it!"

"Yes, sir."

Rockwell leaned back in his seat. Maybe he

would need a second drink.

III

Octobriana stalked through the dark woods with a hunter's guile. She had managed to lose the stormtroopers, but a bad feeling nagged at her.

Thud!

What was that sound?

Thud!

Thud!

Thud!

Whatever it was, it echoed like thunder and was getting closer. She checked the pendant on her shark-toothed necklace. It told her that the radiation levels were rising. There was only one option; to run away from its rapidly approaching source.

Octobriana picked up her pace and cursed her luck. She hadn't even intended on fighting anyone this time. She just wanted to stand guard and see what Criswell's prophecy was all about. Now, she swore that if she got out of this alive, she would strangle George Lincoln Rockwell herself.

Thud!

Thud!

Thud!

The approaching thunder was getting louder by the second. The Russian she-devil kept running until she found herself in a clearing. This wasn't good. There was nowhere left to hide.

Crash!

She turned around to see an enormous white dinosaur smash its way into the clearing, its hungry eyes fixed on her. The creature roared and

Octobriana drew her Smith & Wesson.

Bang!

Bang!

Bang!

The bullets bounced harmlessly off the monster's scaly albino hide. There was only one chance and it was risky.

The dinosaur charged, but Octobriana stood her ground.

Thud!

Thud!

Thud!

The giant monster barreled down on her; its jaws wide open. Now was her chance.

Bang!

She fired a shot into the roof of the creature's mouth, then leapt out of the way. As she landed on the soft grass, her bullet found its way into the dinosaur's brain. It cried out in pain, then rolled over dead.

The Soviet Wonder Woman breathed a sigh of relief and rose to her feet. She could use a cola.

She made her way back through the woods to where the Hatenanny bus waited. But, by the time she made there, it was already too late. George Lincoln Rockwell had been shot by one of his own men.

And, contrary to the claims of various pundits, actual Fascism has made no significant political gains since.

IV

Criswell's dressing room was nothing fancy. He liked it that way. He was styling his hair when, through the reflection in the vanity mirror, he saw his window open and a slim figure with a red star on her forehead slipped inside.

"Gasp," he said, "Octobriana!"

The Russian she-devil aimed her Smith & Wesson at his heart.

"Why?" She asked. Criswell smiled and rose to meet her.

"It's quite simple," he said, "my mission is to kill you."

Criswell took a step forward.

Bang!

The bullet tore through his body. Criswell took another step.

Bang!

Bang!

Octobriana fired round after round into his chest, yet he continued to advance. She aimed at his face and...

Bang!

The skin peeled away, revealing a mass of circuits underneath.

"A robot!" The Soviet Wonder Woman exclaimed.

"Quite right," the man-machine said in a different tone.

"I know that voice," Octobriana declared, "General Malik!"

Malik's voice laughed.

"Do you like Doctor Dimension's latest invention?"

"Not one bit," The Russian she-devil replied, "where's the real Criswell?"

Thump!

That came from the wardrobe! Octobriana rushed towards it and threw open the door. Bound and gagged, the true TV psychic fell into her arms.

"It won't do you any good," Malik warned, "I predict that you will both die in four seconds."

The robot began to glow red hot. With Criswell still in her arms, the Soviet Wonder Woman ducked into the wardrobe and shut the door.

Boom!

The whole building shook as the robot exploded. Was this the end of Octobriana? No, she and Criswell emerged from the rubble battered but alive.

"I guess that's another prediction he got wrong," she said as she removed the gag from her companion's mouth, "tell me, are you really psychic?"

Criswell hung his head in shame.

"I used to have the gift," he said, "I really did. But I lost it when I began accepting money for it."

I

Ricca, the present day...

It is easy to forget that the Cold War never really ended in Asia. When the rest of the world was celebrating the fall of the Iron Curtain, the so-called "Bamboo Curtain" merely tumbled down the memory hole. As a result, Korea remains split to this day. But despite shielding nations such as China and Myanmar, no place is this second curtain of secrecy stronger than the island of Ricca.

Merely a dot on the map, the nation is a manufacturing powerhouse, accounting for twenty-eight percent of the globe's factory labor. There are two key reasons why this number is so high. The first is, despite the ruling party's platform of being the "worker's party", there is an abundance of low-wage workers who may be exploited by foreign companies. Secondly, the factories in Ricca often dismiss health, safety and environmental regulations, which brings the cost of production down. While workplace injury and fatality rates are officially suppressed, the nation remains the world's third largest producer of carbon emissions.

However, neither of these factors have ever prevented American corporations from investing in the Riccan sector. The cornucopia of cheap production has made the island an industrialist's dream. As a result, it is not uncommon to see a laptop or cellphone with the words "Made in Ricca" printed on the outer casing.

Manufacturing ethics be damned, we want our tech!

This became the unofficial slogan of American production in the early twenty-first century. However, that all changed in one fell swoop.

It was a lazy Saturday morning in the United States. The president switched on the television to catch the news. At least, he tried to. The television, you see, simply wouldn't turn on. Annoyed, he decided to check his cellphone instead. Again, the machine simply wouldn't work.

He was not alone in his frustration. All over the country, the populace had woken up to a world without technology. The government tried to convene about the crisis. But, without the communication channels that they were used to, the politicians were effectively scrambling in the dark.

Everything, from phones to cars, had ceased to function. Well, not everything. Tanks drove themselves down the streets while pilotless planes circled every neighborhood.

Then, when the full moon rose, the message came.

Every TV, cellphone and computer sprang to

life at the exact same moment for the exact same purpose.

"This is the Claw," growled a cruel voice, "I am now in control of America's technology. Every weapon, every means of communication and transportation are now mine. Surrender yourselves to my rule or perish."

Yes, the Claw had crawled out from beneath the woodwork once more. And this time, he had the upper hand.

Only one hope remained.

II

While the Wonder Machine waited for her offshore, Octobriana walked stealthily through the jungle of Ricca. She had prey to hunt and she had a feeling that she knew where it was hiding. Black smoke blanketed the entire island and the Soviet Wonder Woman had to wear a gas mask to breathe. As she drew closer to the source of the smoke, she found herself having to wipe toxic filth from the lenses of her mask. Shortly, a looming factory came into view. She peered through the foliage to get a better look at it.

Three smoke stacks reached up to the sky like witch fingers, pumping a thick cloud of toxins into the atmosphere. A barbed wire fence surrounded the building and six guards in gas masks patrolled the outside. Octobriana pondered how she would get inside. Her answer sneaked up behind her.

"Hey you!" said a voice, "why aren't you inside with the other workers?"

The Slavic Superwoman turned around to see a female guard with mask on her face and an M-16 in her hands.

"I got separated from my detail," Octobriana bluffed, "This jungle is a maze. Can you help me?"

The guard eyed her suspiciously. Suddenly, her radio sprang to life. As the Claw's soldier reached to answer it, Octobriana grabbed her dagger and...

Slash!

She cut a slit in her opponent's gas mask. The guard began coughing immediately. She dropped to her knees as she choked on the toxic smoke. Finally, she collapsed dead in the mud. Without a second to spare, the Russian she-devil switched clothes with the guard and carried her corpse up to the gate.

"I killed an intruder," she told the sentries, "I wish to inform the Claw that Octobriana is dead."

The gate opened up for her and the Russian she-devil approached the factory. Another guard at the door let her in, but nothing on the outside could have prepared her for what awaited her within.

The people of Ricca sweated in substandard gas masks, toiling night and day to make trinkets that were designed to malfunction. Men, women and even children risked their health for the crumbs of the First World. The sight made Octobriana sick. But most sickening of all was the giant figure seated in a fiery throne. It gazed down on the turmoil with emerald eyes, which fixed themselves on the Slavic Superwoman.

Octobriana approached the Claw with guarded thoughts, for she remembered that he was a mind-reader.

"I believe you have good news?" He asked. She nodded and lay the corpse on the floor. The God of Hate studied the body keenly.

"Those clothes," he said, "can it be that this is the mighty Octobriana? Oh joyous day! First, I am victorious in America. Then, my most hated foe is slain. You shall be rewarded dearly. But first, I wish to see Octobriana's face..."

He reached down and, with a single talon from his giant hand, he removed the gas mask

from the guard's corpse. The Claw paused. The
Soviet Wonder Woman took advantage of his
momentary confusion and...

Bang!

She shot out the lights and the factory was
plunged into blackness. Octobriana threw a
grenade at the Claw and...

Kaboom!

She didn't see if it killed him or not. She didn't
wait to find out either. She threw another grenade
at the door and...

Kaboom!

It blew a giant hole in the wall.

"Everybody out," she said, "head for the
waterfront. The Wonder Machine will rescue you
there."

She watched as the workers all raced out of
the factory, trampling the guards in one enormous
stampede. However, her moment of victory was
short lived. A gigantic hand came out of the
darkness and grabbed her.

"Fool," said the Claw, "did you really think
that you could kill the God of Hate? At last,
Octobriana, I'm finally rid of you."

He brought her up towards his jaws, which
opened hungrily.

That line, Octobriana thought, *that's what the
old man said. I'm not actually here. None of this is
real. I'm still in the book shop. I must out of here...*

The Slavic Superwoman pulled the pin from
one last grenade.

"Eat this!" She said as she tossed it into the
Claw's mouth.

Kaboom...

Back in the book shop, the Slavic Superwoman tumbled out of the paperback world and into reality. The man in the Mickey Mouse mask seemed surprised to see her again. Octobriana drew her Smith & Wesson and pointed it between his eyes.

"Who are you?" She demanded. With his mask on, she couldn't tell if he was smiling or not. However, she had the impression that he was grinning.

"Who am I?" He asked rhetorically, "only your oldest foe. We've never been formally introduced, but I've been there from the very beginning. Now, know my true form!"

Mystic vapors surrounded him and Octobriana watched him morph into something monstrous. When the mist at last parted, he had changed into an enormous, satanic figure dressed in green with a dollar sign on his chest. The Slavic Superwoman gasped.

"The Green Manalishi!" She exclaimed, "I should have known. But why? Why the book?"

"Fool," the dollar devil replied, "as much as you are a woman, you are also a symbol. I thought that if I co-opted that symbol and mass produced it for easy consumption, I could rob it of its potency. *The Hunger Games*, *V For Vendetta*, heck, even *Star Wars* are effectively Octobriana-Lite. Stories like that convince the audience that they are proletariats, fighting valiantly against the evil Galactic Empire and, thus, that framing dominates the modern political narrative. Ask anyone on any side of the political aisle and they will tell you that they are a rebel. In truth, though, there are no more revolutionaries. There are only demographics, special groups, which may be exploited for profit. And so, these Rebels (TM) spend an obscene amount of their hard-earned money on Guy Fawkes masks, toy lightsabers, mocking jay pins and so on, all in aid of feeling like their fictional revolutionary heroes. In reality, by investing in these stories and all related merchandise, they are directly supporting the very system that they think they are rebelling against. They are supporting me."

The Green Manalishi laughed. Octobriana cocked her pistol and pulled the trigger.

Bang!

No effect.

"What?" The dollar devil said, "did you really think I could be stopped with bullets? I am a part of human society, of human nature. No mere weapon can harm me. Don't you even feel the desire to consume more than you need?"

"No," Octobriana replied, "because now that I've seen your true colors, I can recognize you for what you are."

She holstered her gun.

"And that recognition is the true weapon against you."

The Green Manalishi snarled.

"Curse you, Octobriana. Our paths will cross again!"

He vanished in a flash of hellfire. Now it was the Slavic Superwoman's turn to laugh.

"I'm counting on it," she said.

The End